Woody pointed to the poster about skating lessons hanging in the window. "Look! There's only one spot left. Only one more person can sign up."

"So?" Randi said.

"So, sign up!" Anna cried.

Randi's mouth dropped open. She stared at her two friends. "What? You know I can't sign up. Mom won't let me!"

"But you have to! This is your last chance to skate with us!" Anna exclaimed. "We need just one more kid to start the class." Anna and Woody pointed at Randi. "*You!*"

Don't miss any of the fun titles in the Silver Blades

FIGURE EIGHTS series!

ICE DREAMS
STAR FOR A DAY

and coming soon:

THE BEST ICE SHOW EVER!
BOSSY ANNA

Ice Dreams

Effin Older

Created by Parachute Press

A SKYLARK BOOK
NEW YORK • TORONTO • LONDON • SYDNEY • AUCKLAND

RL 2.6, 006–009

ICE DREAMS

A Skylark Book / March 1996

ISBN 0-553-48491-5

Published simultaneously in the United States and Canada

PRINTED IN THE UNITED STATES OF AMERICA

OPM   0 9 8 7 6 5 4 3 2 1

This book is for Jules.

1

Ice Skating Star?

"And now, ladies and gentlemen, our final skater. From Grandview Elementary School . . . introducing eight-year-old Randi Wong!"

Randi stared out across the glassy ice of the Seneca Hills Ice Arena. The bleachers were filled with people. Hundreds of people. *They're all looking right at me,* she thought. *What if I fall? What if I forget my routine?*

Randi smoothed the ruffles on her purple skirt.

She checked the purple bows on her long black pigtails.

She took a deep breath and stepped onto the ice.

"This is it," Randi whispered to herself. "My big chance."

Randi glided to the center of the rink. She slid to a stop. The crowd became quiet. Everyone was waiting. The bright lights of the Seneca Hills Ice Arena dimmed. A single spotlight fell on Randi.

Forget all those people, Randi told herself. *Forget everything except skating.*

Randi raised both arms over her head. She tucked one skate behind the other. She waited for the music on her tape to start. All she could hear was the loud *thump, thump, thump* of her heart.

Then the music began.

Randi took off. She circled. She twirled. She jumped. She danced.

Randi's spins were whirlwinds. Her splits were scissors. Her hardest jump of all—the double axel—was as easy as one, two, three.

The audience cheered. They clapped in time to the music and shouted, "Ran-dee! Ran-dee!"

Then the music ended.

Randi bowed to the audience and to the judges. A giant smile spread across her face.

One of the judges walked onto the ice. She placed a crown of daisies on Randi's head. "This is for you—our new champion," she said.

Randi giggled with delight.

"What's so funny?" Randi heard someone say.

Randi laughed harder. Her shoulders shook. The daisy crown fell from her head.

"Hey! Randi! What's so funny?"

It was Woody Bowen. Woody's real name was Forrest, but everyone called him Woody. Everyone except his mother. Woody had green eyes and a face full of freckles. His red hair always looked messy. His wrinkled, oversized shirt and baggy jeans looked as if he had slept in them.

Woody's voice surprised Randi.

Randi looked at Woody and touched the top of her head. "My daisy crown. Where's my . . . ?"

"What daisy crown? Randi, what are you talking about?"

Randi patted her straight black hair. She blinked her big brown eyes. She glanced down at her blue-and-white-striped shirt and denim overalls. And then she shook her head and looked around.

She was sitting on the top bleacher, row 22 of the Seneca Hills Ice Arena. Her violin case and her backpack lay next to her. Far below on the ice, Randi's fifteen-year-old sister, Jill, was practicing jumps with the Silver Blades skating club.

There was no cheering audience.

No daisy crown.

No polished white skates with silver blades on her feet.

Randi looked up at Woody and smiled. "I was daydreaming that I was skating."

4

Woody shrugged. "You're always day-dreaming, Randi." He flopped down beside her on the bleacher. "I've been looking for you. Want to hear a knock-knock joke?"

Woody and Randi were in the same third-grade class at Grandview Elementary. Woody had to spend a lot of time at the ice arena. His mother was president of the Silver Blades skating club. Silver Blades was a club for really good skaters. Randi's sister Jill and Woody's older brother, Mitchell, were in the club.

Mrs. Bowen always had a lot of paperwork to do in the rink's office, so Woody had to come right to the rink after school.

Randi spent a lot of time at the ice arena, too. Jill brought her to the rink four days a week after school. Jill was the oldest in their family. It was her job to look after Randi while their parents worked.

Randi complained a lot that eight years old was way too old to have a baby-sitter. But she really liked hanging out at the rink. It was tons more fun than practicing the violin. While Jill practiced skating, Randi played with Woody. Sometimes she even did her homework. But most of the time she and Woody roamed around the arena.

Next to the figure-skating rink and the ice hockey rink were Harry's Snack Bar and Mr. Mullen's pro shop. There was also a weight room, an aerobics room, and some offices, where Woody's mother worked. There were two big locker rooms, one for boys and one for girls. Randi and Woody knew every inch of the Seneca Hills Ice Arena. It was their playground.

"So, do you want to hear my joke or not?"

"Sure," Randi said. She knew she'd hear it even if she said no. Woody told jokes all the time.

"Knock knock," Woody said.

"Who's there?"

"B.C."

"B.C. who?" Randi asked.

"Be seeing you!"

Randi laughed. "Good one, Woody."

"So, what are you doing?" Woody asked.

Randi flipped her long black hair off her shoulder. "Nothing. I'm just watching Jill practice. What are you doing?"

"Nothing," Woody said. "I'm waiting for my mom. Hey, let's race around the bleachers!"

Suddenly Randi's stomach growled. "I'm too hungry to run right now," she said. "And I don't have any money to buy something to eat. I spent the last of my allowance. Do you have any money?"

Woody took off his backpack. He never went anywhere without it. He unzipped a small pocket and dug around in it. He came up with a dime and two pennies.

"Twelve cents?" Randi asked. "Is that all?"

"Okay, okay, I'll look again." Woody unzipped three other pockets. Then he turned the backpack upside down and shook it. Out fell a six-foot-long paper-clip chain, a water pistol, and a Slinky. The Slinky immediately slunk down all twenty-two bleacher steps. As Randi and Woody watched it, more stuff tumbled out of Woody's backpack: two finger puppets, a

bicycle horn, a live snail and a book about snails, and one, two, three, four, five wrinkled sheets of paper.

"Want to see something neat?" Woody asked, forgetting about the money. He picked up a sheet of paper. On it was a picture of a hand.

"A hand? So what?" Randi said.

"This is not just any old hand. This is *my* hand," Woody said. "I copied my own hand on Mom's copy machine. Cool, huh? Next I'm going to copy my head, my feet, my—"

"Woody, I'm still hungry!" Randi said.

"Oh, yeah, I forgot. Let's go to the snack bar. Maybe Harry will sell us twelve cents' worth of fries."

"Six cents' worth each," Randi moaned. "We'll probably only get two fries for that." She picked up her violin case and her backpack. Her stomach growled again—a long, loud, gurgly growl.

"Twenty-one, twenty, nineteen, eighteen . . ." Randi and Woody yelled out the numbers of each row as they raced down the bleacher steps. At the bottom they found the Slinky under a seat. Woody slipped it into his backpack, and they headed toward the snack bar.

When they passed the rink, Randi saw Jill practicing her jumps. Randi stopped as Jill spun into the air—once, twice—and then landed, gliding smoothly back onto the ice.

"That looks so cool," Randi said to Woody. "Someday I'm going to be the one jumping and spinning on the ice. Just the way I saw it in my dream!"

2

Meet Moo and Shmoo

Randi and Woody stared at the sign in the window of Harry's Snack Bar. Randi could not believe it: CLOSED. BACK IN 30 MINUTES.

"No way!" Randi cried. "I can't wait half an hour. I'm starving!"

"Let's try the pro shop," Woody suggested. "They have chocolate bars. Maybe they have a twelve-cent size."

"Okay," Randi said. "I hope Anna is there."

Anna Mullen was one of Randi's best friends. She was nine and in the fourth grade at Grandview Elementary. Anna's parents were divorced, and Anna lived with her father. He owned the pro shop. Anna always came right to the rink after school, too. Anna, Woody, and Randi had been playing at the rink since they were four years old. They were known as Triple Trouble.

When Randi and Woody ran up, Mr. Mullen was taping a poster to the front window of the pro shop.

"Hi, Mr. Mullen!" Randi cried. She waved to him.

"Hi, Randi. Hi, Woody," Mr. Mullen called. "Anna is inside."

Randi liked the pro shop. It had everything ice skaters needed—new skates, skates for rent, laces, sweatshirts, leotards, warm-up suits. Mr. Mullen also sharpened and fixed skates.

"Look! Anna's over there!" Randi yelled and pointed to the back of the store. Anna's long, curly brown hair was peeking out over the top of a huge cardboard box. Randi and Woody rushed over.

Randi noticed that Anna was wearing yellow sweats and a matching yellow top with a panda bear on the front. Her outfit looked brand-new.

Anna is so lucky, Randi thought. *She gets so many neat new outfits from her father's shop.*

Randi was used to hand-me-downs. She had six brothers and sisters.

"Hi, Anna," Woody said. "What are you doing?"

Anna rolled her blue eyes. "Dad said I have to put all these T-shirts on the shelves or I can't have a new outfit. I'll probably be a hundred years old before I finish."

"We'll help," Woody said. He poked Randi. "Won't we, Randi?"

Randi peered into the box. It was filled with black, white, and red T-shirts that all said SENECA HILLS ICE ARENA.

"I'm too hungry to help!" Randi exclaimed. Then she said to Anna, "Do you think we can buy a chocolate bar for twelve cents?"

"I don't know," Anna replied. "Ask Dad."

Randi ran outside. Mr. Mullen was straightening the poster he was hanging.

"Hi again, kiddo!" he greeted Randi when she came up to him.

Randi looked up at Mr. Mullen. "I'm really hungry, and I spent my allowance. I was wondering, um, well, do you have a chocolate bar for twelve cents?"

Mr. Mullen scratched his head. "I'm sorry, Randi. Chocolate bars are fifty-five cents or more."

Randi slowly walked back to her friends. "Twelve cents is nowhere near enough. We need at least fifty-five cents," she told them. "I guess I'll go ask Jill."

"Wait!" Anna said. "I have an idea! We'll make a deal with Dad. I'll tell him you'll help me put T-shirts on the shelves. When we're finished, Dad will give us each a chocolate bar."

"Okay," Randi said. "That's great! We'll do it, won't we, Woody? Please?"

Woody grinned. "Okay. Go ask him, Anna."

"Dad! Could you come over here a minute, please?"

"I'm coming," Mr. Mullen said.

Anna groaned. "I can't do all these T-shirts by myself. Randi and Woody said they would help me if—" She stopped and looked up at her father hopefully.

"If what?"

"If they can each have a chocolate bar. Puhlease, Dad."

Her father stared into the box. He looked at Anna. He looked at Randi and Woody. Then he laughed. "Okay, Anna, we have a deal. I'll never sell these shirts if they stay in the box. As soon as the job is done, you can each pick out a chocolate bar."

Randi couldn't wait. "Excuse me, Mr. Mullen," she said politely, "but I need the chocolate bar *now*. Can we have our chocolate bars first? I'm starving!"

"All right," Mr. Mullen said. "But there better not be one chocolate smudge on any of those nice new T-shirts."

"We promise," Randi, Woody, and Anna said all together.

Anna picked a chocolate bar with nuts. Woody picked one with raisins. Randi chose her favorite: nuts *and* raisins.

They each took an enormous bite.

Then Anna said, "Here's what we'll do. Randi, you're the shortest. You start to stack T-shirts on the bottom shelf. I'm the tallest. I'll stack T-shirts on the top shelf. Woody, you're in the middle. So you do the middle shelf."

"You got it, Bossy Anna," Woody said. He saluted Anna and marched over to the box of T-shirts.

Randi started to giggle. She put her hand over her mouth. Woody was right; Anna was bossy. But it didn't bother Randi. She knew Anna wasn't mean. Her plan to stack T-shirts was a good one. And Anna was the one who had figured out how to get the candy bars!

Randi carefully placed three shirts on the bottom shelf—one white, one red, one black. Woody grabbed a whole bunch of shirts. He flopped them down onto the middle shelf.

Anna stacked four white shirts neatly, one on top of the other.

Woody was reaching for another bunch when Anna yelled, "Woody, these shirts are not neat! Dad won't like it. Here, I'll show you how to stack shirts properly."

"Oh, great! You do it. Stacking shirts is too boring!" Woody dropped a whole armful of shirts on the floor.

"It may be boring, Woody, but a deal is a deal," Anna said sharply.

"I want to make a *new* deal," Woody said.

"You can't make a new deal," Randi said.

"Yes, I can! This is my new deal. You two do the shirts. And I'll put on a show."

Woody picked up his backpack and disappeared behind a rack of warm-up pants. In a minute his hands appeared above the rack. On each hand was a finger puppet. The puppets were bright green with wild orange hair and big red eyes. Randi thought they looked like little aliens from outer space.

Hiding behind the rack, Woody wagged a finger. "Meet Moo." One little puppet bowed. Then he wagged a finger on the other hand. "This is Shmoo. They will tell you a joke."

In a high, squeaky voice Moo said, "Knock knock."

In a deep voice Shmoo answered, "Who's there?"

"Annie," Moo squeaked.

"Annie who?" Shmoo growled.

"Annie-body hungry?"

Randi and Anna fell down laughing.

"Okay, Woody, you have a deal," Anna said. "We'll stack the T-shirts. But one knock-knock joke isn't enough. You'll have to do twenty jokes."

"Right! And they all can't be knock-knock jokes," Randi said. She took another bite from her chocolate bar.

"Okay. Here's a scratch-scratch joke." Woody wiggled his Shmoo finger. "Scratch scratch."

"Who's there?" Moo asked in a high, squeaky voice.

"M-two," Shmoo said in a deep voice.

"M-two who?" Moo asked.

"M-two tired to knock!"

Anna and Randi laughed even harder.

Randi laughed so hard, she spit out a whole mouthful of candy. Melted chocolate globs, half-chewed sticky nuts, and little black raisins flew out of her mouth.

A big glob landed on Anna's sweatpants.

A little glob landed on Woody's shoes.

And worst of all, two of the biggest, wettest globs landed on one of Mr. Mullen's brand-new, never-been-worn, white-as-snow T-shirts!

Anna and Woody watched Randi. Their eyes were wide. Their mouths dropped open.

Randi turned as red as a beet. She wished she could jump into the box of T-shirts and never come out.

3
Violin Forever
and Ever

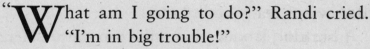

"What am I going to do?" Randi cried. "I'm in big trouble!"

"Oh, no!" Anna yelled. "Wait till Dad sees this!"

"Oh, gross!" Woody yelled.

Mr. Mullen heard their cries. He headed to the back of the shop. "What's all the fuss about?" he asked.

Randi tried to hide the chocolate-stained shirt behind her back. But she had to tell the truth. Randi could hear her heart pounding as she held the T-shirt up for Mr. Mullen.

"It's just this one shirt, Mr. Mullen," Randi said in a tiny voice. "I'm really sorry."

"You aren't sick, are you, Randi?" Mr. Mullen asked. He ruffled her hair. Randi shook her head.

"Don't worry, Randi. It's only a shirt. There are hundreds more." Mr. Mullen laughed. "Why don't you kids forget the stacking for today?"

Randi could hardly believe it! He wasn't mad! "Thanks, Mr. Mullen!" she said. Anna's dad was a really cool father.

Just then Jill walked into the pro shop. "Here you are," she said to Randi. "I'm done with practice. It's time to go home."

"See ya," Randi called to Anna and Woody. She followed Jill out of the pro shop.

And then suddenly she saw it.

Randi stopped in her tracks. She stared up at the poster Mr. Mullen had taped to the door. She read the poster. Then she read it again:

NEW! NEW! NEW!
GROUP ICE SKATING LESSONS

**7- to 9-YEAR-OLDS
EIGHT STUDENTS PER GROUP
SIGN UP BELOW**

At the bottom of the poster Randi read *Send your check for $60 to Carol Crandall at the Seneca Hills Ice Arena.*

"Oh, wow!" Randi cried. Her dream could come true. She could take skating lessons! "Look, Jill," Randi said, pointing at the poster. "Skating lessons for kids my age! Can I sign up?"

"I don't know," Jill replied. "You'll have to check with Mom and Dad."

Randi stared at the poster. She wanted to sign up now. Right now!

"Come on!" Jill called. "We have to go. I have homework to do."

Randi gave the poster one long last look. "I'm going to ask Mom and Dad the minute we get home. The very minute!" she squealed.

"Randi! Wait!" It was Mr. Mullen.

Uh-oh. I'm in trouble now, Randi thought. *Mr. Mullen must have changed his mind about the T-shirt!*

But when Randi turned around, she saw that Mr. Mullen was holding her backpack and her violin case.

"Oops, I forgot," she said, as he handed her things to her.

Randi was relieved—Mr. Mullen really wasn't angry. But she wished she had lost her violin forever. She hated that violin. She hated violin lessons with old Mr. Campton. More than anything, she wanted to take skating lessons. And now there were going to be lessons for kids her age—right there at the arena!

Right then Randi decided to ask her parents if she could quit violin. She would take skating lessons instead. Her parents would see what a good idea skating was. Yes! Her mind was made up. She would do it at dinner that night.

Suddenly Randi felt good all over. Today was

her lucky day! *Good-bye, violin! Hello, skating!*

"Hi, girls," Mrs. Wong greeted Randi and Jill when they got home. "I was beginning to wonder where you were."

"Sorry, Mom," Jill said. "I lost track of the time. I practiced my jumps for two hours straight."

"Practice makes perfect," Mrs. Wong said. "Dinner's ready." She set a big bowl of salad on the dining room table.

Randi loved dinnertime. The whole noisy Wong family got together and everyone talked about what he or she had done that day.

Randi sat next to Jill. Henry, Randi's twelve-year-old brother, sat across from her. Henry the Horrible, Randi sometimes called him. Henry played soccer. He always wore his soccer shirt. Always! He thought it was bad luck to wash it. Henry thought he was so cool.

Kristi sat next to Henry. She was ten. Kristi

always had her head stuck in a science book. Kristi wanted to be famous and discover something important someday—maybe the cure for hiccups!

The twins, Michael and Mark, sat on either side of Mr. Wong. They were six, and right now they were totally into being firefighters. They were always carrying pretend hoses while they ran all over the house putting out make-believe fires. They were really cute.

Three-year-old Laurie was the youngest. She was pretty good at talking. But she still called Randi Wandi.

Once dinner began, Mrs. Wong always said, "So, how was everybody's day?"

Then the noise started. Everyone spoke at once.

"I made two—" Henry blurted.

"I don't want—" Randi began.

And every day Mr. Wong would tap his spoon on his glass and say, "Quiet now." Everyone would turn to him, waiting.

Pick me. Pick me, Randi thought.

"Henry, let's hear about your day first," Mr. Wong said.

Oh, poo! thought Randi.

"I scored two goals today," Henry said. He tapped himself on the chest. "My last goal broke the tie. And we won the game."

Mrs. Wong reached over and patted Henry's arm. "We're so proud of you, Henry."

My turn, my turn, Randi thought. She jiggled nervously in her chair. *I'll say good-bye to violin lessons forever!*

But Mr. Wong said, "Kristi is next. How about you, Kristi?"

"I'm going to run for president of the geology club."

"Good for you," Mr. Wong said. "I hope you win."

I wonder what geology is, thought Randi.

At last Mr. Wong turned to Randi. "So, Randi, what have you been up to?"

Randi looked up. Now that she had everyone's attention, she didn't know what to say. What if her parents didn't let her quit violin?

What if they said she couldn't take skating lessons? She sat in her chair silently.

"Randi, are you learning any new songs on the violin?" Mrs. Wong asked.

Randi shrugged. "Not really. I've been thinking. . . ." She paused. Everyone was watching her. "I've been thinking I'd like to try something else besides the violin. Something that's more fun."

"Well, Randi, one after-school activity for each of you is all we can afford," Mr. Wong said gently.

"I'm not asking to have two activities," Randi said quickly. "I want to give up violin." She paused. "I want to skate."

There! I said it! she thought.

"Randi can't skate! We all have to do something different, don't we?" Henry whined. "It's a Wong rule, isn't it?"

"Keep quiet, Henry. It's not your turn," Randi snapped. Henry could be such a pain.

But Henry was right. It was a Wong family rule that each of the kids have a different after-

28

school activity. Mr. and Mrs. Wong believed that each of their children would have some- thing special that way. Randi used to like the rule. It made her feel special. Now she wasn't so sure.

"Randi," Mrs. Wong said, "Jill chose skating a long time ago. You chose the violin. You have only been playing for two years. I'm sure if you wait a few more years you will love playing beautiful music."

Randi blinked away the tears that filled her eyes. She didn't want to practice the violin one more day.

Jill put her arm around Randi's shoulder. "Don't look so sad. Skating isn't all fun. You have to get up really early and practice every day. Even when you don't feel like it."

But Randi didn't cheer up. *This is not my lucky day,* she said to herself. *It's yucky-violin-forever day!*

4
Cover Your Ears!

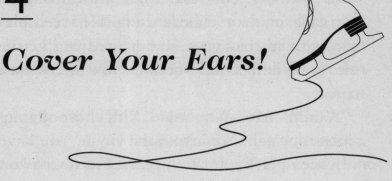

"Hey, Randi! Want a nice, gooey chocolate bar?" Max Harper teased. He was sitting on the front steps of Grandview Elementary with Woody and Anna.

Randi looked at Anna and Woody. "You told everyone in school about the shirt, didn't you?"

Anna shook her head.

Woody said, "I only told Max."

Max pushed a strand of blond hair out of his eyes. "I wish I had seen it! Scientifically speaking, you erupted like a volcano!"

Max was always saying "scientifically speaking." He was nine and in Anna's fourth-grade class. Science was Max's thing. He loved playing with microscopes and magnifying glasses. He even had a mini–science lab in his basement.

"Randi erupted, all right!" Woody exclaimed. "All over my shoes!"

Randi glared at Woody. "Do you have to keep talking about it?"

"Talking about what?"

Randi turned to see her good friend Kate Alvaro. Kate sat down beside Randi. She was wearing a green hat with a big sunflower on the front. It matched her green checked vest and short green skirt. Kate and Randi had been friends since nursery school.

Woody said, "I was talking about how Randi spit chocolate and nuts and—"

"Wood-eee!"

Woody paid no attention to Randi. He told the whole story about the shirt. Everybody burst out laughing—everybody except Randi.

"It may be funny to you," Randi said, "but it

was scary to me. Luckily, Mr. Mullen wasn't mad."

Kate said, "That wasn't half as scary as the time I hit the umpire in the head with the bat! When it comes to sports, just call me Kate the Klutz." She rolled her eyes. "But Mom keeps signing me up. She thinks sports are good for me."

"There's a poster in Dad's shop about group skating lessons," Anna said. "I'm going to sign up right away!"

"Me too!" Woody said. He pretended to skate across the step. "I could really fly on blades!"

"I would be terrible at skating," Kate moaned. "Don't tell Mom or else she'll sign me up for sure!"

"You're lucky, Kate," Randi said. "My mother won't let me sign up." She made a face. "Just because I chose the violin when I was still a baby and didn't know better, I have to like it now. Yuck!"

The school bell rang. Randi, Woody, and

Kate raced to the third-grade room. Anna and Max ran off to the fourth-grade room.

After school, Anna, Randi, and Woody met on the front steps. They met there every day except Mondays—that was when Randi stayed after school for her private violin lessons.

Today was not a violin lesson day, and they were waiting for Woody's mother to pick them up and take them to the ice arena. Some days Jill walked over from the middle school and took them all on the bus to the rink.

At the rink, the three friends climbed up to the top bleacher. It was their favorite place. They watched the Silver Blades skaters practicing.

"Look at Mitchell!" Woody cried. "My brother is sure an awesome skater."

"Not as awesome as Jill," Randi replied. "Jill is going to be in the Olympics someday. I just know it! I wish I could jump and spin and twirl like that."

"You can!" Anna declared. "We all can! We can sign up for the group skating lessons right now. You and Woody and me. We'll learn to skate together. It will be so cool!"

"Cool for you," Randi said sadly. "Uncool for me." She poked her violin case with her toe. "I'm stuck with this dumb old thing, remember? I'm supposed to practice an hour every day. I hate it!"

"Hey, I've never heard you play. You should practice right now," Woody suggested. "Anna and I can be your audience."

"Okay, but you have to promise not to laugh."

Woody and Anna promised.

Randi opened the case. She tucked the violin under her chin. "I'll play 'Twinkle, Twinkle, Little Star,' " she said. "It's my best song."

Randi placed the bow on the strings and pulled.

Squ-aawk! Scr-eech! Squ-eeal!

"Wow!" Woody yelled. "That is really terrible!" He clamped his hands over his ears.

"This is torture!" Anna shrieked.

Randi stopped playing. She looked down at the ice. She noticed that even some of the skaters were covering their ears.

"I think it's much worse in the rink because of the echo," she explained.

"Does your mother ever listen to you practice?" Anna asked.

Randi shrugged. "Not really. I mostly practice in the rec room in the basement—so I won't bother anybody."

All of a sudden Anna's eyes grew big. "I know how you can quit violin. Forever! For sure!"

Randi knew Anna could come up with great ideas. But this one would have to be *fantastic*!

"Your mother is coming to pick you and Jill up this afternoon, right?" Anna said.

Randi nodded. "Yes. So what?"

Anna motioned to Randi and Woody to come closer. Randi couldn't wait to hear Anna's plan!

* * *

An hour later, Randi spotted her mother coming through the doors of the skating rink. "Up here, Mom!" Randi shouted, and waved.

Mrs. Wong climbed to the top bleacher, where Randi, Anna, and Woody were sitting. Randi's violin lay on her lap.

"What are you doing?" Mrs. Wong asked. She sat next to Randi.

"Randi has been practicing her violin," Anna replied. She gave Randi a secret smile.

"Want to hear my new song, Mom?" Randi asked her mother.

Mrs. Wong smiled. "I would love to, honey."

Randi tucked the violin under her chin. She glanced at Anna and Woody. They were trying not to giggle.

Anna's plan was about to begin.

Randi pulled the bow s-l-o-w-l-y, oh so s-l-o-w-l-y, across the violin strings. The sound echoed all over the arena.

Squ-aaaawk! Scr-eeeech! Squ-eeeeal!

Randi continued to play. She concentrated

on playing the notes—even though they were the wrong ones.

Squ-aaaawk! Scr-eeeech! Squ-eeeeal!

Down below on the ice, everything stopped. The Silver Blades skaters grabbed their ears. Two skaters fell down. One skater crashed into the boards. People from all over ran into the rink to see who was making such horrible sounds.

Kathy, the Silver Blades coach, started climbing the bleachers. She hollered up to Randi, "Stop! Stop that terrible noise!"

But Randi played on and on. *Mom might not think my violin playing is bad enough,* she thought. She played more wrong notes.

"Please, Mrs. Wong," Kathy begged. "Please tell Randi to stop playing, *right now*!"

Mrs. Wong yelled into Randi's ear, "Stop, Randi!"

Randi finally stopped.

She glanced at Anna and Woody. Their faces were bright red. They were trying to hold in their laughter. Randi's playing was horrible. Worse than horrible.

"Well, Mom, how did I do? Did you like it?" Randi asked. She smiled sweetly.

Mrs. Wong swallowed hard. "Well . . . it was . . . well, I know you were trying, honey. You know, Randi, I've been thinking. . . ."

Randi's stomach suddenly felt full of butter-flies. Had the plan worked? Did her mother see that violin lessons were a waste of time?

"I think we need to talk about your violin lessons," Mrs. Wong finally said.

Randi jumped up. "Do you mean it, Mom?"

"Not now," Mrs. Wong said. "We have to be getting home. We will discuss it later."

Randi kept her fingers crossed all the way home.

5
Fat Chance

Randi didn't say another word about the violin or skating as they drove home. She just kept hoping that Anna's plan had worked. Maybe now her mom would let her quit the violin—and join the skating group.

But Mrs. Wong didn't say anything more about it. By dinnertime, Randi was a wreck!

"Mom!" Henry yelled. "Randi is picking at her food!"

Randi shot Henry a look. "That's none of your business!" she snapped.

Everybody was talking about what he or she had done that day. Randi didn't hear a word anyone said. She was wondering if her parents had talked about her lessons yet. She wanted to shout, "Did you make up your minds? Can I quit?" But she didn't dare.

After dinner, Randi helped dry the dishes . . . without being asked.

She did her homework . . . without being reminded.

She cleaned her room . . . without being told.

I'm being so good, they'll have to let me take skating lessons, she thought.

Mr. Wong gave the twins a bath. Mrs. Wong read a bedtime story to Laurie. Then they sat down in the living room to watch the evening news. Still no one said a word about violin lessons.

"So much for being good!" Randi muttered. "They've forgotten all about me! I wish I hadn't dried those dumb old dishes!" She stormed upstairs.

"Hey! What's your problem?" Jill called from her bedroom. Jill was curled up on her bed reading *Skating* magazine.

"Nothing," Randi grumbled. *Jill can't help me,* she thought on her way to her room. *Nobody can.*

Randi stomped into the bedroom she shared with Laurie. She got into her pajamas and crawled into bed. She hugged Big Six, her teddy bear. Big Six had been a present for her sixth birthday. "You would let me quit violin, wouldn't you, Big Six?" Randi whispered.

With a little help from Randi, Big Six nodded.

"Nobody cares about me," Randi complained. "Nobody cares that I want to skate more than anything in the whole wide world."

Randi was about to turn off her reading light when she heard a tap on the door. In walked her parents. "Randi, you forgot to kiss us good-night," Mrs. Wong said. "We've come for our good-night kiss."

"We have been discussing your violin lessons," her father began.

"You have?" Randi cried, sitting up straight. Under the blanket, she crossed her fingers.

Mrs. Wong smoothed Randi's hair. "Yes, honey. And we have decided that . . ."

Randi held her breath. She squeezed her eyes shut tight, hoping, hoping, hoping.

Mrs. Wong smiled. "We have decided that you are a very brave little girl. It took a lot of courage to play your violin in front of all those people at the ice rink. Not many eight-year-olds would do that."

"And we are very proud of you for wanting to play your violin in public," Mr. Wong added. "Keep up the good work and one day we'll come to see you in a concert hall."

"But . . . but . . . ," Randi began. Under the blanket, her fingers slowly uncrossed. "You mean . . . you didn't come to tell me I can quit violin?" She tried not to cry, but she could feel tears filling her eyes. "You mean I can't take skating lessons? I have to stay with violin?"

Mrs. Wong sat down on Randi's bed. "Randi, honey," she said, "if you give up the violin, you'll be skating in Jill's shadow."

Randi swallowed the big lump that suddenly filled her throat. "Jill's shadow?" she repeated. "What do you mean?"

"What your mother means is that Jill is a very talented skater. Skating is more to Jill than an after-school activity. We don't want to see you compare yourself to Jill. The violin is yours alone."

"One day you will be as good at violin as Jill is at skating," Mrs. Wong said. "Because you love music so much!"

"No, I don't. I don't love music at all. And I hate the violin!" Randi cried.

"You've always been good at music," her father said. "Remember in kindergarten when you won an award for being the best recorder player in the class? Your mother and I knew then that music would be your talent."

"But, Dad, that was the recorder!" Randi exclaimed. "I was a baby then. The violin is different. It's not fun. Not anymore."

"Honey, we think you need to give it more time," her mother said. "Now try to get some sleep. We love you." She tucked the covers around Randi.

Anna's plan hadn't worked. In fact, it had backfired. Randi's parents were *proud* that she had played at the rink.

Randi sank down in her bed and pulled the blanket over her head. Salty tears dropped onto Big Six's fuzzy face. "Now what am I going to do, Big Six? Now what am I going to do?"

"Pssst! Randi!"

Randi wiped her tears and peeked out over the blanket.

Jill stood in the doorway in her pajamas. "I heard what Mom and Dad said. I'm really sorry, Randi. Maybe someday they'll change their minds."

"Fat chance!" Randi muttered.

But Randi was not giving up. She had to find a way to make her parents see how much she wanted to skate. She just had to.

6

The Very Last Spot

The next afternoon, Jill took Randi to the ice arena. As they passed the pro shop, Randi spotted Kate and her mother inside. Randi said, "Kate's terrible at sports. What is she doing in there?"

"Go in and find out. See you later." Jill dashed off to practice, and Randi hurried into the pro shop.

"Hi, Randi!" Kate called. "Can you believe it? Mom signed me up for skating lessons! Watch out, everybody!"

Kate—Kate the Klutz—was trying on skates!

"You mean . . . you mean you're going to Carol's lessons, too?" Randi asked.

"Yes. With Anna and Woody and Max. They're over there, trying on skates. Hurry up and get yours!"

It was bad enough that Anna and Woody were skating without her. Now Kate and Max were skating, too?

"Hey, Randi! Look at me!" Max called. Mr. Mullen was tightening the laces on Max's new black skates. "Mom wants me to do something besides science," he said. "I bet I'll be a good skater. I tried it once at my cousin's birthday party. I was slick!"

Mr. Mullen winked. "Show us how slick you really are, Max. Stand up!"

Max slid off the bench. He stood up . . . for one second. Then he wobbled like a bowl of Jell-O and fell to the floor.

Everybody laughed.

"Guess you could use a lesson or two," Mr. Mullen said. "Who's next?"

"Me!" Woody yelled.

"Then me!" Anna added.

"Then me!" Randi said. Only she didn't really say it. She just wished it.

Randi watched as all her friends tried on their new skates. She had never felt so left out in her entire life. Violin lessons were lonely— just Randi, old Mr. Campton, and the violin. Skating lessons with her friends would be fun.

"I can't stand everybody getting skates but me," Randi said to Anna. "I'm going to watch Jill practice." She started out of the pro shop.

"Wait, Randi!" Woody yelled. "I have to show you something." He grabbed Randi's hand and pulled her to the front of the shop. Anna followed right behind them. Woody pointed to the poster—the skating lessons poster hanging in the window. "Look! There's only one spot left. Only one more person can sign up."

"So?" Randi said.

"So, sign up!" Anna cried.

Randi's mouth dropped open. She stared at

her two friends. "What? You know I can't sign up. Mom won't let me!"

"But you have to! This is your last chance to skate with us!" Anna exclaimed. "We need just one more kid to start the class." Anna and Woody pointed at Randi. *We want you!*

Randi shook her head. "No way! Mom will ground me forever."

"No, she won't," Woody said. "You can explain to her that there was only one spot left. One spot. And you took it. When she hears how much you want to skate, she'll change her mind"—he snapped his fingers—"just like that!"

Randi shook her head. "I don't think so."

"Go on, Randi!" Woody said.

Randi stared at the empty space on the poster. *Do it, Randi!* whispered a little voice inside her head. But another little voice whispered, *Don't do it, Randi!*

"Please, Randi," Anna begged. "Then we'll all be together!"

Randi looked at her friends. She looked at the poster. She stared at the empty space. She took a deep breath.

Slowly, ever so slowly, Randi picked up the pen hanging beside the poster. In teeny-tiny letters she printed one word—*Randi*. Then she printed a second word—*Wong*. Then she stood back and stared at her name on the last line of the poster.

Uh-oh, Randi thought. *Now what have I done?*

7

A Close Call

Randi thought hard about how to tell her parents that she had signed up for skating lessons.

She thought about it all through dinner that night.

She thought about it before she went to bed.

She thought about it when she fell asleep.

She was still thinking about it the next morning.

And then the phone rang.

"I'll get it!" Henry said, jumping out of his chair at the breakfast table. "It's probably about soccer practice." He answered the phone, then quickly handed it to Mrs. Wong. "It's some woman from the ice rink. Something about Randi and skating lessons." He made a face.

Oh, no! Randi sank down in her chair. *Now I'm in trouble!*

"Hello," Mrs. Wong said into the phone. "Yes, I'm Randi Wong's mother. . . . Skating lessons? Oh, I think you mean Randi's sister, Jill. . . . Money? What money?" Mrs. Wong rolled her eyes impatiently.

Randi could feel her ears getting hot and her cheeks turning pink. If only she had told her mother about the lessons herself. Now it was too late!

"Yes, I'm certain there's been some mistake," Mrs. Wong said into the phone. "Thank you very much for calling. Good-bye."

Mrs. Wong hung up the phone. She shook her head. "Sometimes they get so mixed up down there at the rink. Okay, kids. Ready for school?"

Whew! Randi thought. *That was close!*

Randi felt great . . . for a minute. Then she remembered something. She remembered that it didn't matter if her name was on the skating list. She couldn't take lessons without her parents' permission. Her parents would never give permission. Or pay for the lessons.

I have to tell Mom, Randi scolded herself. *But I have to find the perfect time!*

All day long Randi thought about how she should tell her mom about the skating lessons. She had to tell the whole truth, but in a really nice way—so she wouldn't get into trouble. And, more important, so she wouldn't ruin her chance to take skating lessons.

Randi decided she would bring it up when her mom came to get her at the rink.

After school, Randi waited for Jill. But when Jill came, they didn't go to the rink. Jill's skating practice had been canceled.

That meant Randi's plan to talk to her mom at the rink was canceled, too.

As Randi and Jill walked home, Randi came up with a new idea—the perfect idea!

I know. I'll use my own money to pay for the lessons. Then Mom and Dad can't say no. They'll have to let me take skating lessons. No problem!

When they reached the house, Randi ran up to her room. She shut her bedroom door. Laurie was still at day care with the twins. And Kristi and Henry were at after-school activities. But to be extra safe, Randi dragged her desk chair across the room. She put it in front of the door.

Then she lay down on her stomach and wriggled under her bed. Her piggy bank was hidden under an old sweatshirt, next to a very large dustball. She grabbed the bank and crawled out from under the bed.

Randi stared at the bank. It was in the shape of a pig's head. She turned the bank over and pulled out the plastic plug. Then she shook it. Coins and dollar bills fell all over the floor.

Randi scrambled to pick them up. She began to count.

She had to count three times, because she kept messing up.

Her heart sank. "Twenty-three dollars and forty-six cents," she told Big Six. "I need sixty dollars for the lessons. I need a lot more money."

Where could she get the rest of the money?

"I have to get a job," Randi told Big Six.

She thought about what kind of job she should get. Sometimes she helped Henry shovel snow off driveways in the winter, and the neighbors paid her. Randi looked out the window. The sun was shining. There was no snow. Bad idea.

"I've got it!" she cried. "A lemonade stand."

She pulled the chair back to the desk. She opened her bedroom door and ran downstairs. Jill was in the den, watching music videos. Randi hurried into the kitchen.

She opened the refrigerator. No lemons. She

opened the cabinets. No lemonade mix. She searched the entire kitchen. All she could find was a container of milk. Would any kid buy plain old milk from a stand? Randi didn't think so.

Randi glanced at the clock. It was almost five-thirty. Her mother would be home soon to make dinner. Randi had to think of something fast.

She wished Anna were here. Anna would know how to make money in a hurry. But Anna was with her father in the rink's pro shop.

The pro shop! That's it! Randi thought.

Randi would call Mr. Mullen. He would give her a job.

Randi hurried to the phone on the desk in the kitchen. She looked at the list of important phone numbers her mother kept by the desk. She found the number for the Seneca Hills Ice Arena and dialed. When someone answered the phone at the rink, Randi asked for Mr. Mullen in the pro shop.

"Hello," Mr. Mullen said into the phone.

"Hi, Mr. Mullen. It's Randi. Randi Wong."

"Hi, Randi. Wait a minute, I'll go find Anna for you."

"Uh, no, Mr. Mullen. I—uh—wanted to talk to you." Randi could hear her voice shaking. "I was wondering—could you give me a job?"

"A job?" Anna's father asked.

"Yeah," Randi said. "I could stack shirts for you. And then you can pay me."

Mr. Mullen laughed. "I'm sorry, Randi. I can't give you a job. And remember what happened the last time you tried to stack shirts?"

"But that was an accident!" Randi cried. "I promise I won't get any chocolate on the shirts if you give me a job. Really, I won't!"

Mr. Mullen laughed again. "Randi, you're too young to work. I can't give you a job."

"Oh," Randi said. She didn't know what else to say. And then she heard her mother's car pull into the driveway.

"Thanks. Bye!" Randi blurted into the phone. She quickly hung up and bolted for her bedroom. She didn't want to talk to her mother just yet. She still had to figure out the best way to tell her about the lessons.

8

Awfully Big Trouble

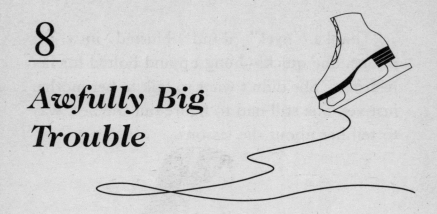

All the Wongs sat down to eat dinner that night. Henry spent most of the meal pleading with their father to buy them a dog. Mr. Wong kept saying no. Randi concentrated on eating her chicken. She tried not to look at her parents. After dinner, Kristi cleared the dishes, and Jill brought out dessert. It was Randi's favorite—cookies-'n'-cream ice cream.

Now is the perfect time to tell them, Randi thought. But before she could say anything, Mrs. Wong said, "I stopped by the ice arena on my way home from work to pay for Jill's new warm-up jacket. While I was there, I ran into Carol Crandall, the new skating instructor."

Randi gulped. Had Carol told her mother about the sign-up sheet? Had she asked her mother for the money?

"I know Carol," Jill said. "She's nice. She's the instructor for those new lessons for younger kids." Jill glanced at Randi. "Remember? It was on that poster in the pro shop."

Randi stared at her plate. "I know," she squeaked.

Mr. Wong cleared his throat.

Uh-oh, Randi thought, *that's what he always does before he has something big to say.*

He looked straight at Randi. "Do you have something you would like to tell us, Randi? Something about the skating lessons?"

Randi burst out, "I can explain everything! I really can!"

Mrs. Wong folded her arms. "I certainly hope so."

"I don't know what's going on, but this I have to hear!" Henry said, grinning from ear to ear.

Randi narrowed her eyes at Henry. Then she

said to her parents, "I tried to tell you! I really did. But you were always too busy, or . . ." She looked down at the brown-and-white ice cream melting in her dish. "Or I was too scared."

"What did Randi do now, Mom? What did she do?" Henry asked excitedly.

Mrs. Wong didn't answer. She looked at Randi. "Carol told me you signed up for her skating lessons. Is that true?"

Randi nodded a teeny-tiny nod.

"Wow!" Henry said.

Randi felt like throwing her soupy ice cream at Henry. But she was in enough trouble already. "Yes, I signed up!" she blurted. "I had to! There was only one spot left! It was my last chance! All my friends at the rink are skating. Everybody! Anna, Woody, Max. Even Kate the Klutz! I'm the only one left out. I don't want to be left out. I don't want to take violin lessons all by myself. I want to skate—more than anything!" The words came tumbling out of Randi's mouth.

Mrs. Wong raised one eyebrow. "It doesn't matter what all your friends are doing, Randi. You know you should have asked us first."

Randi nodded.

"I really hope you never, ever do anything like this again," Mr. Wong added.

"I'm sorry," Randi said softly. She kept her eyes on the ice cream.

Mrs. Wong took a sip of coffee. Then she said, "We are not happy with this, Randi. And just because you've signed up for lessons doesn't mean you can take them!"

Randi nodded again.

Mr. Wong said, "After dinner, go straight to your room. Do your homework and practice your violin. And no TV. Your mother and I will have to talk about this. Do you understand?"

"Yes," Randi said. She pushed her chair away from the table. "May I please be excused now? I'm not hungry."

Her father nodded.

Randi trudged upstairs. She threw herself onto her bed. "Oh, Big Six!" she cried. "I've messed up everything! Everything! Now I'll never skate. What am I going to do?"

Big Six just stared at her with his big brown button eyes.

Randi did ten subtraction problems and played "Twinkle, Twinkle, Little Star" four times on her violin. Then she changed into her nightgown and crawled into bed. She heard a knock on her door. It was Jill. "Want some company?" Jill asked.

"Okay," Randi answered.

Jill sat cross-legged at the foot of Randi's bed. "Mom and Dad are really mad," she said. "You shouldn't have signed up without asking them."

Randi let out a big sigh. "I know, but it was my only chance. They don't understand. I even tried to get a job to pay for the lessons. I want to skate more than anything."

"Skating looks easy," Jill said, "but it's tons of hard work. It's not all fun, Randi."

"I know, but I still want to skate," Randi said. "I really, really do!"

Jill slid off the bed. "You're just like me. You don't give up easily," she said. "Okay. How about if I say something to Mom and Dad? Maybe I can make them understand how much you want to skate."

Randi's face brightened. "Would you, Jill? Would you, please?"

"I'll try. But they're still angry," Jill warned. "No promises."

Randi threw her arms around Jill. "You're the best big sister in the whole wide world!" she cried.

Jill hugged Randi. "Good night," she said as she closed the door softly behind her.

"Please let Mom and Dad listen to Jill," Randi whispered in the darkness. "If they don't . . ."

But Randi didn't even want to think about that!

9

Look at Me!

The next morning Randi woke up early. Her eyes were still half closed as she stumbled to the bathroom. On the way, she passed Jill's bedroom. The door was open, and Jill's bed was neatly made. *Jill's at skating practice already,* Randi thought. *She left without telling me what Mom and Dad said. That means it's bad news.*

Randi shuffled back to her room. "This is going to be the worst day of my life," she muttered. "I'm getting back into bed and never getting out. Not to eat. Not to go to school. Not for anything!"

Randi climbed into bed and was about to

pull the blanket over her head when she noticed something.

It was sitting at the foot of her bed.

It looked like a shoe box, only bigger.

"Probably some of Laurie's toys," Randi grumbled. "She's always leaving her junk on my bed."

Randi nudged the box off the bed with her foot. As it crashed to the floor, the lid popped off. When she saw what was inside, she couldn't believe her eyes.

"Skates!" she cried. "Beautiful white skates!"

Tucked inside one of the skates was a note:

Dear Randi,
These are for you. I won my first competition in them. I hope they bring you good luck.

Love,
Jill

Randi closed her eyes and hugged the polished white skates. "Thank you, Jill," she whispered. "Thank you."

Randi was so excited about the skates that she almost didn't see the envelope taped to the lid of the box. She tore it open. Inside was another note:

Dear Randi,
We had a long talk with Jill last night. She convinced us that you want to skate as much as she did when she was your age. You've also shown us that when you set your mind to something, you can stick with it!

Here's the check for your skating lessons. Have fun with your friends. You have lots of hard work ahead.

Hugs and kisses,
Mom and Dad

"Yippee!" Randi shouted. She waved the check in front of her teddy bear. "Look, Big Six! This is the best day of my life!"

She ran downstairs and gave her mother a

big hug and lots of kisses. "You're the best mother in the whole world!" Randi told her.

Anna, Woody, Max, and Kate were already on the ice when Randi's mother dropped her off at the rink. Three other kids from Randi's third-grade class were there, too.

Max skated slowly in one direction. He took little steps and hung on to the rail with one hand. Anna and Kate stood in the middle of the rink. They held hands and took short glides. Woody was on his hands and knees, trying to stand up. They were all laughing and shouting and having fun.

"Yay! Your parents let you skate with us!" Anna yelled when she spotted Randi. "Hurry up! Put on your skates! This is the best!"

Randi laced her skates and stood up. She smiled a really big smile. *Look at me, everybody!* she said to herself. *I'm a skater!* She took off the plastic guards on the bottoms of her skates and stepped onto the ice.

"Watch out! It's slippery!" Woody yelled.

Randi stood still. She didn't try to move. She felt the cold, hard ice under her skates and dreamed that she was gliding gracefully across the shiny surface.

"Ready for your lesson?" asked a voice behind her.

Randi snapped out of her daydream.

"Hi. I'm Carol Crandall." Carol had a long black ponytail. She was wearing a red warm-up jacket over a blue leotard. She was holding the sign-up poster. "Aren't you Jill Wong's little sister?" she asked.

"Yes," Randi said proudly. "Jill is in Silver Blades."

Woody crawled across the ice on his hands and knees. "I'm Woody Bowen," he said as Carol helped him up. "My brother, Mitchell, is in Silver Blades, too."

Carol gathered all eight skaters around her. "Let's see who we have here," she said, running her finger down the list of names. "I've just met Randi and Woody. Now, everybody else, please raise your hand when I call your name."

Kate, Anna, and then Max raised their hands. So did Josh Freeman, Samantha Rivers, and Frederika Hamilton.

"Does our group have a name?" Anna asked Carol.

"A name?" Carol asked. "What do you mean?"

"A club name," Randi said. "Like Silver Blades. Can we be called Silver Blades, too?"

"Yeah," Woody agreed. "We need a cool name."

"Hmmm," Carol said. "We have eight skaters. I have an idea. Let's call ourselves the Silver Blades Figure Eights."

"Yay! The Silver Blades Figure Eights!" all eight skaters shouted. Randi shouted loudest of all.

The rink was cold, but Randi felt warm all over. "I'm in Silver Blades Figure Eights," she whispered. "My dream has come true!"

If you glided right through SILVER BLADES FIG-
URE EIGHTS, jump into the SILVER BLADES se-
ries, featuring Randi Wong's big sister Jill and her
friends. Look for these titles at your bookstore or
library:

BREAKING THE ICE
IN THE SPOTLIGHT
THE COMPETITION
GOING FOR THE GOLD
THE PERFECT PAIR
SKATING CAMP
THE ICE PRINCESS
RUMORS AT THE RINK
SPRING BREAK
CENTER ICE
A SURPRISE TWIST
THE WINNING SPIRIT
THE BIG AUDITION
NUTCRACKER ON ICE
RINKSIDE ROMANCE
A NEW MOVE

and coming soon:

ICE MAGIC